# Hole Help

Illustrated by The Artful Doodlers

Random House New York
Thomas the Tank Engine & Friends™

CREATED BY BRITT ALLCROFT

Based on The Railway Series by The Reverend W Awdry. © 2010 Gullane (Thomas) LLC.
Thomas the Tank Engine & Friends and Thomas & Friends are trademarks of Gullane (Thomas) Limited.
HIT and the HIT Entertainment logo are trademarks of HIT Entertainment Limited.
All rights reserved. Published in the United States by Random House Children's Books, a division of Random House, Inc., 1745 Broadway, New York, NY 10019, and in Canada by Random House of Canada Limited, Toronto. Step into Reading, Random House, and the Random House colophon are registered trademarks of Random House, Inc.
www.stepintoreading.com    www.randomhouse.com/kids    www.thomasandfriends.com

Educators and librarians, for a variety of teaching tools, visit us at
www.randomhouse.com/teachers
ISBN: 978-0-375-85368-5    MANUFACTURED IN CHINA

HiT entertainment

"Where is Thomas?"

says Emily.

Emily wants Thomas.

Where is Thomas?

Look!

Thomas hid.

"Rugs!"

says Emily.

"That is not Thomas."

Emily wants Thomas.

Where is Thomas?

Look!

Thomas hid.

"Logs!"
says Emily.
"That is not Thomas."
Emily wants Thomas.

A hole!

Emily has hit a rock.

Emily is in a hole.

"Where is Emily?"

says Thomas.

Thomas can go to Emily.

Thomas wants to help.

Thomas can help.

Emily is out of the hole.